PRESIDENTS DAY

HOLIDAYS

Lynda Sorensen

The Rourke Press, Inc.
Vero Beach, Florida 32964

© 1994 The Rourke Press, Inc.

All rights reserved. No part of this book may be reproduced or utilized in any form or by any means, electronic or mechanical including photocopying, recording or by any information storage and retrieval system without permission in writing from the publisher.

Edited by Sandra A. Robinson

PHOTO CREDITS
© Gene Ahrens: cover, pages 10, 12, 13, 15; © Frank Balthis: page 21; courtesy Illinois Department of Commerce and Community Affairs: title page; courtesy Lincoln Boyhood National Memorial: page 4; courtesy National Park Service: pages 7, 8; courtesy Lincoln Home National Historic Site: page 17; courtesy U.S. Army Military History Institute: page 18

Library of Congress Cataloging-in-Publication Data

Sorensen, Lynda, 1953-
   Presidents Day / Lynda Sorenson.
      p. cm. — (Holidays)
   Includes index.
   ISBN 1-57103-073-5
   1. Presidents' Day—Juvenile literature I. Title.
II. Series: Sorensen, Lynda, 1953-   Holidays.
E176.8.S65   1994
394.2'61—dc20   94-3354
                                                              CIP
                                                               AC

Printed in the USA

TABLE OF CONTENTS

Presidents Day	5
George Washington	6
General Washington	9
President Washington	11
Honoring George Washington	14
Abraham Lincoln	16
President Lincoln	19
Honoring Abraham Lincoln	20
Celebrating Presidents Day	22
Glossary	23
Index	24

PRESIDENTS DAY

Presidents Day is a **national** holiday that honors two of America's greatest presidents, George Washington and Abraham Lincoln.

Both Washington and Lincoln were born in February. Washington was born on February 22, 1732. Lincoln was born on February 12, 1809. Presidents Day celebrates both birthdays on the third Monday of each February.

Presidents Day is a legal holiday in most states. A few states, however, still celebrate the birthdays of Washington and Lincoln on separate days.

Abraham Lincoln's boyhood home is visited by thousands of Americans each year

GEORGE WASHINGTON

Americans remember George Washington with great respect. Washington worked and fought to help America become a free, **independent** nation.

Henry Lee, an army officer who served under Washington, described General Washington as "First in war, first in peace and first in the hearts of his countrymen."

George Washington, America's first president, is often called "the father of our country."

This is George Washington in a painting by Rembrandt Peale

GENERAL WASHINGTON

Americans fought the Revolutionary War (1775-1783) to earn freedom from England. George Washington became commander-in-chief of the Continental Army in 1775. His army of American colonists fought the English soldiers.

George Washington bravely and skillfully led the Continental Army. With great difficulty, he and his army finally won the war. The United States became a free and independent nation.

George Washington poses in his Revolutionary War uniform in a painting by James Peale

PRESIDENT WASHINGTON

In 1789 George Washington was elected the first president of the new United States of America. President Washington helped form the nation's first government.

Washington was elected to a second term in 1793. In 1797 he retired to his family home, Mount Vernon, near the Potomac River in Virginia.

The statue of Washington on a horse stands at the Ford Mansion, Washington's wartime headquarters in Morristown, New Jersey

Soon after the terrible Civil War battle at Gettysburg, Pennsylvania, President Lincoln stood on the battlefield and praised the soldiers' bravery

George Washington retired to his home, Mount Vernon, in Virginia

HONORING GEORGE WASHINGTON

Washington, D.C., the capital of the United States, is named in honor of George Washington. The Washington Monument in Washington, D.C., honors the nation's first president, too. The 555-foot-tall, needle-shaped tower is the tallest structure in the capital.

Washington is also honored as the only president to have had a state named after him.

George Washington is always nearby. His picture is on quarters and one-dollar bills.

The Washington Monument glows in floodlights in Washington, D.C.

ABRAHAM LINCOLN

Abraham Lincoln was a man of courage and wisdom. He was America's president during a very difficult time, the Civil War of 1861-1865.

During President Lincoln's time, landowners in America's Southern states owned black people as slaves. Most people in the North wanted to **abolish,** or do away with, slavery.

The Southern states felt their way of life was being threatened by the North. They decided to break away from the rest of the United States.

Abraham Lincoln led the North during the Civil War of 1861-1865

PRESIDENT LINCOLN

President Lincoln ordered the Army to keep the Southern states from breaking away. The states went to war against each other, North against South. During the Civil War, in 1863, Lincoln gave an order that freed all slaves. It was called the **Emancipation** Proclamation.

After four years of terrible bloodshed, the South surrendered on April 9, 1865. Before President Lincoln could begin to heal the nation's wounds, he was murdered on April 14, 1865.

In a field tent, President Lincoln (left) discusses the war's progress in 1861 with General McClellan, a general he later fired

HONORING ABRAHAM LINCOLN

Many cities, towns, streets, schools and parks throughout the United States are named for Abraham Lincoln.

In Washington, D.C., the Lincoln Memorial honors the 16th president. The Lincoln Memorial is a white marble building surrounded by 36 columns. A huge statue of President Lincoln is inside, and the Emancipation Proclamation is engraved on a wall.

Lincoln is remembered as the "Great Emancipator" — the one who ordered freedom for all people. His face is on the penny and five-dollar bill.

The Lincoln Memorial in Washington, D.C., honors the "Great Emancipator"

CELEBRATING PRESIDENTS DAY

Presidents Day honors two men who worked hard for America during difficult times. All U.S. government offices, such as the Postal Service offices, are closed on Presidents Day. Many schools are also closed. During February, school children learn more about the remarkable lives of George Washington and Abraham Lincoln.

Glossary

abolish (uh BAHL ish) — to do away with; to eliminate

emancipation (eh man suh PAY shun) — freedom from the control of others

independent (in deh PEN dent) — free; not controlled by others

national (NAH shun ul) — of or relating to a nation

INDEX

Civil War 16, 19
Continental Army 9
Emancipation Proclamation
    19, 20
England 9
English soldiers 9
February 5, 22
Great Emancipator, the 20
Lee, Henry 6
Lincoln, Abraham 5, 16, 19,
    20, 22
Lincoln Memorial 20
Mount Vernon 11
North (the) 16, 19
Potomac River 11
Revolutionary War 9
slavery 16
slaves 16, 19
South (the) 19
states 19
    Southern 16, 19
Virginia 11
Washington, D.C. 14, 20
Washington, George 5, 6, 9,
    11, 14, 22
Washington Monument 14